This book belongs to

....

This is the story of Three Billy Goats Gruff.

You can read it yourself – it's not very tough.

Why not have a try, if you're brave enough!

One thing more. Can you guess what?

On every page there's a worm to spot!

Three Billy Goats Gruff

Nick and Claire Page

Illustrations by Katie Saunders

make
believe
ideas

In the valley, by a river,
lived three happy billy goats:
Little Will,
Brother Bill,
and Rough Tough Gruff.

On the mountain, by a bridge,
lived a nasty troll called Sid.
He had eyes as big as pies,
ears like two big saucepan lids,
yellow teeth, and a wrinkly throat!
His favorite food was goat.

One fine day, there was not
much grass in the valley.
"It's time to go," said Little Will.
"Let's cross the bridge to the
higher ground, where there's
lots of grass around."

Keep off

Do Not enter

So the three goats trotted
off to the bridge.
"I'll go first," said Little Will.
Trip-trap-trip! As he ran,
Sid the Troll jumped out and sang...

"I don't want bacon,
I don't want lamb,
I don't want turkey,
I don't want ham.
I don't want chicken,
or beef, or pork.
I want some goat
upon my fork!"

Keep off

Little Will smiled sweetly and said:
"Don't have me for your tea;
I am not much good to eat.
To fill your insides,
why not try some Goat Surprise?"

"Goat Surprise?" said the troll.
"Oooh, that sounds completely yummy!"
"Well, you'll soon have some in your
tummy," said Little Will.
"My big brother can tell you more."

Next, Brother Bill came along.
Trip-trap-trip! As he ran,
Sid the Troll jumped out and sang...

Stay off or else

No trespassing

"I don't want apples,
I don't want cherries,
I don't want peaches,
I don't want berries.
I don't want plums,
or grapes, or prunes.
I want some goat
upon my spoon!"

Brother Bill stood still and said:
"Don't have me for your tea;
have some Goat Surprise instead."

"Goat Surprise?" said the troll.
"That sounds absolutely great!"
"In a moment," said Brother Bill,
"you will have some on your plate!
My big brother will be here.
All you have to do is wait."

Rough Tough Gruff appeared,
and ran onto the bridge.
Trip-trap-trip! As he ran,
Sid the Troll jumped
out and sang...

18

"I don't want lettuce,
I don't want beans,
I don't want cabbage,
I don't want greens.
I don't want carrots,
peas, or shallots!
I want some goat
here in my pot!"

Rough Tough Gruff stood still and said:
"Pick on someone your own size!
Here's my special Goat Surprise!"

"Goat Surprise?" cried the troll.
"Oooooh, it's mine at last!"
Rough Tough Gruff charged at Sid
and gave him a mighty kick.
Sid felt sick.

Rough Tough Gruff and Bill and Will
made their home on the grassy hill.
Sid the Troll disappeared.
All his friends said he was ill.
From then on, his friends took note,
Sid could not stand the taste of goat.

Do not
enter

Ready to tell

Oh no! Some of the pictures from this story have been mixed up! Can you retell the story and point to each picture in the correct order?

Picture dictionary

Encourage your child to read these harder
words from the story and gradually develop
their basic vocabulary.

bridge

goat

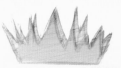

grass

kick

mountain

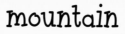

river

troll

valley

worm

Key words

Here are some key words used in context. Help your child to use other words from the border in simple sentences.

The goats **like** grass.

Bill stood **on** the bridge.

"Goat is **my** favorite dinner!"

Gruff charged **at** him.

Grow a grassy meadow

The three billy goats wanted to get up to the good grass on the green meadow. Here's how to grow a beautiful "meadow" that you can enjoy eating.

You will need

a new face cloth, or about ten sheets of paper towel
• a large plate or plastic tray • mustard and cress seeds
• scissors • a spoon

What to do

1 Put the face cloth or paper towel in a pile on the plate or tray. Soak the cloth or paper by spooning cold water onto it.

2 Sprinkle mustard and cress seeds over the damp cloth or paper.

3 Put the plate or tray on a sunny windowsill.

4 Sprinkle with water each day so the paper doesn't dry out. At the same time you can see if your seeds are starting to sprout shoots.

5 After a few days your "meadow" will be covered in green mustard and cress "grass" that's ready to harvest. Use the scissors to cut off as much as you need. Mustard and cress taste very good in egg salad sandwiches. You could probably even eat it with roast goat – but don't tell Sid the Troll!